Mr. FLUX

With love to Mr. Yoshi, Mr. Mika, Mr. Milo & Mr. Oren

And very special thanks to Matte, Yvette, Karen P and Tara — K.M.

For my Vivienne, who has been my best friend now for so many years I have lost count, and who kept asking me when I was going to be finished with this book — M.S.

Kids Can Press acknowledges the financial support of the Government of Ontario, through the Ontario Media Development Corporation's Ontario Book Initiative; the Ontario Arts Council; the Canada Council for the Arts; and the Government of Canada, through the CBF, for our publishing activity.

Published in Canada by
Kids Can Press Ltd.
25 Dockside Drive
Toronto, ON M5A 0B5

Published in the U.S. by
Kids Can Press Ltd.
2250 Military Road
Tonawanda, NY 14150

www.kidscanpress.com

The artwork in this book was rendered in gouache.
The text is set in Bauer Bodoni and ROMP.

Acquired by Tara Walker
Edited by Yvette Ghione
Designed by Karen Powers

This book is smyth sewn casebound.
Manufactured in Shenzhen, China, in 12/2012
through Asia Pacific Offset

CM 13 0 9 8 7 6 5 4 3 2 1

**Library and Archives Canada Cataloguing
in Publication**

Maclear, Kyo, 1970–

Mr. Flux / written by Kyo Maclear ; illustrated by Matte Stephens.

ISBN 978-1-55453-781-5 (bound)

I. Stephens, Matte II. Title.

PS8625.L435M57 2013   jC813'.6   C2012-905188-8

Kids Can Press is a *corus*™ Entertainment company

Mr. FLUX

written by
Kyo Maclear

illustrated by
Matte Stephens

Kids Can Press

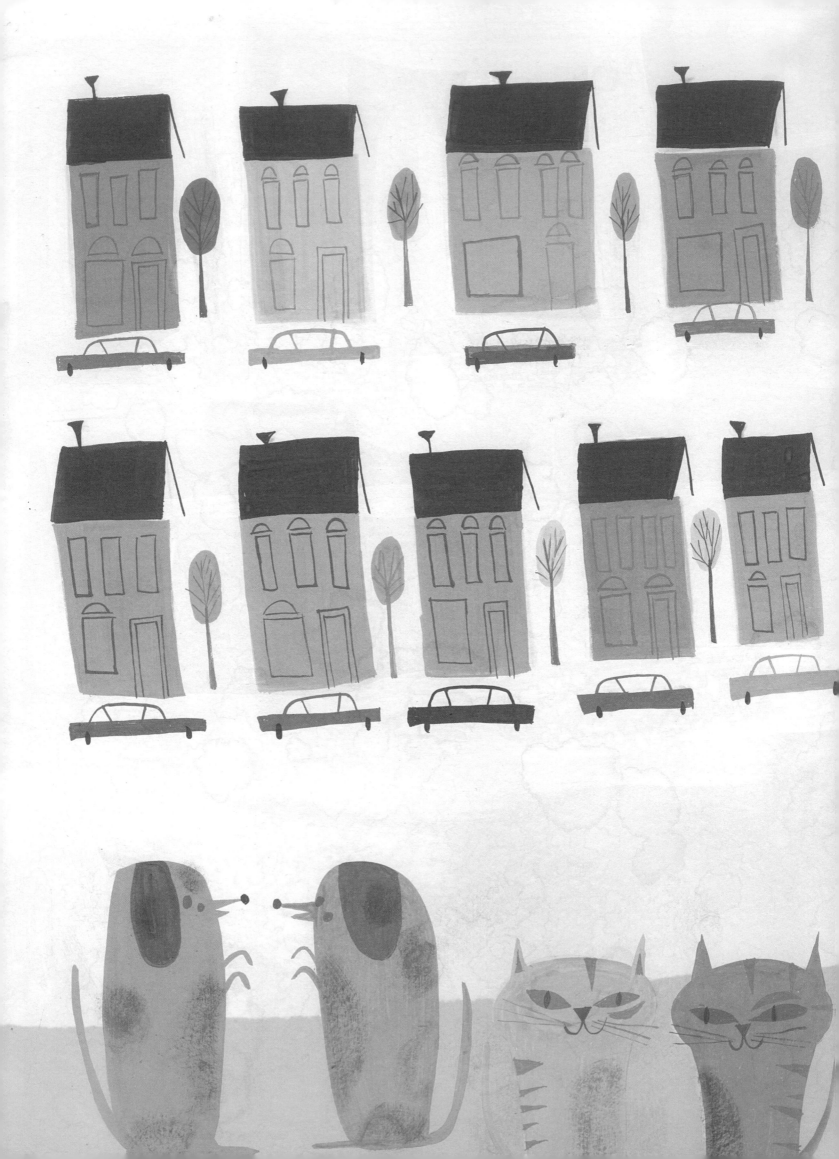

There was once a boy named Martin who didn't like change.

Actually, it wasn't that he didn't *like* change, but more that he didn't *know* change.

He lived with his family in a square house set in the middle of an unchanging street with a fixed number of trees, dogs, cats and cars.

It was a very nice but predictable place.

That is until a man named Mr. Flux arrived
one afternoon out of nowhere in a noisy old van.
Mr. Flux didn't just *know* change, he *loved* it.
He walked around wearing a bowler hat and
called himself an artist even though he didn't
make drawings or paintings or
sculptures or anything
remotely art-like.

While others were busy making
sure everything stayed the same,
Mr. Flux enjoyed mixing things up.

"That crazy artist," said Martin's dad.
"What could he possibly be thinking?" said his mother.

And so it went, with each day seeming to pass like every other day. Until one morning when Martin was riding home on his old red bicycle (his new red bicycle being too new and scary to ride), and the day took a sharp and unexpected turn. There, right in the middle of his path, sat a large wooden box.

He noticed PROPERTY OF MR. FLUX printed on one side and, since Martin was a good neighbor, he knew what he had to do. He set his bike aside and carried the box to Mr. Flux's house and knocked three times.

Almost instantly the door flew open, and there
stood Mr. Flux in his bowler hat and pajamas.
　"My name is Martin," said Martin. "I found your box."
　"Hello, Martin. Look, my friend just
sent me a bit of sky," said Mr. Flux,
holding up a blue puzzle piece.

"Did you know that I have a phone collection and a tuba filled with tennis balls?" said Mr. Flux.

"Don't you want it?" asked Martin, holding out the box.

Mr. Flux looked at the box and shook his head. "No. You should keep it."

"But what's in it?"

"Why, it's full of change," said Mr. Flux.

"Oh," said Martin, and he thanked Mr. Flux politely. He didn't want to open it. (He suspected it contained cacophony, disorder and germs.) But he didn't want to get rid of it, either. So Martin headed home with the large wooden box on his handlebars.

What a commotion that caused.

"Oh, dear. What next?" said one man.

"Heavens to Murgatroyd," said another.

Martin looked around at the crowd of worried and unhappy faces gazing over the hedges and knew what he had to do.

He returned to Mr. Flux's house and knocked on the door.

"You can have your box back. We don't like change around here."

"Oh?" said Mr. Flux. "And why is that?"

"Because change is upsetting, and we like things just the way they are."

"I see. But, Martin, everything changes. Look around you. A dewdrop, a bubble, a cloud. What stays the same?"

"I'm not talking about teensy-weensy changes."

"Right. Well," said Mr. Flux, taking the wooden box from Martin, "can I offer you a jelly donut instead? Or perhaps a ride in my plane? Or shall we spin toy rabbits on my record player?"

By the time Martin returned home he had tried six new things.

The next morning, Martin put on a shirt he had never worn before.

At breakfast, he skipped the Crazy Crackles and ate toast instead.

When Martin's mother saw him, she had an idea to do the same.

Martin had decided that little
changes were okay, but not big changes
like riding his new bicycle.

Over the next few days, he visited Mr. Flux often. Sometimes Mr. Flux would talk about his ideas.

CHANGE IS TO KEEP US ON OUR TOES. CHANGE IS TO MAKE US LOOK MORE CLOSELY.

YOU CAN MAKE CHANGE OR IT CAN MAKE YOU!

WHAT DOESN'T CHANGE ARE THE ARMS YOU USE TO HUG WITH. THOSE STAY THE SAME.

Sometimes Martin would try to teach Mr. Flux how to make art the right way. Martin showed Mr. Flux that some artists made things that actually looked like something.

And Mr. Flux showed Martin that other artists made things people didn't see as art but that could still make you feel wonderful.

And even though Martin was sometimes confused and Mr. Flux was sometimes puzzled, they both liked each other enough to give new things a go.

As time passed, the neighbors began to notice Mr. Flux's influence on the street.

A few houses magically changed color.

One family awoke to find the town mayor eating apples on a ladder in the middle of their lawn.

And another discovered the local
librarian tossing salad in their wading pool.
  Children began to wake up early,
hoping to spot something new.
  The most surprising change
was in people's thinking.

Then one day Martin woke up to a big change.
Mr. Flux was moving away.
Martin had grown used to Mr. Flux. What if he
left and nothing ever changed again?

The day Mr. Flux was to leave,
his van broke down.
Martin was secretly happy. But
then he saw Mr. Flux's sad face
and knew he had places to go.

So while Mr. Flux tried to fix his van, Martin snuck off to fetch his beloved old red bicycle.

It was a bit small for Mr. Flux, but after a few adjustments, he was on his way.

Just before he left, he gave Martin the wooden box.
This time, Martin brought it home …
where he finally opened it.

Pesos and yen. Francs and liras.
There was change from all over the world.
Martin read the note taped to the box
and smiled.

Sometimes change is BIG
and sometimes it's SMALL and
sometimes change is JUST CHANGE
and that's fine, too.
Thank you for the art lessons!

A Note from the Author

The character of Mr. Flux is very loosely based on a man named George Maciunas. He was a Fluxus artist. In fact, he came up with the name "Fluxus," which is really just a fancy word for change.

Fluxus was an art movement that started in the early 1960s. It brought together artists, filmmakers and musicians from all over the world who shared a love of humor and playfulness and change. As one artist named Dick Higgins put it, Fluxus started when people woke up one morning and said, "Hey! Coffee cups can be more beautiful than fancy sculptures. A kiss in the morning can be more dramatic than a drama by Mr. Fancypants. The sloshing of my foot in my wet boot sounds more beautiful than fancy organ music …"

Sound crazy? Well, maybe it was. Fluxus didn't take art or life too seriously. It was meant to be fun and simple. Sometimes the artists made art that couldn't be seen. Sometimes the musicians played instruments that couldn't be heard. Mostly, they believed in friendship and in doing beautiful and crazy things that would invite people to look at the world around them in a new way.